CHEEKY CHICK
and friends

PIPPBROOK BOOKS

First published in 2000
This edition produced in 2013 for Indigo Books Canada
by Pippbrook Books,
an imprint of The Templar Company Limited,
Deepdene Lodge, Deepdene Avenue, Dorking, RH5 4AT, UK
www.templarco.co.uk

1 3 5 7 9 10 8 6 4 2
1112 008

ISBN 978-1-84877-990-7

Designed by Manhar Chauhan
Edited by Liza Miller

Printed in China

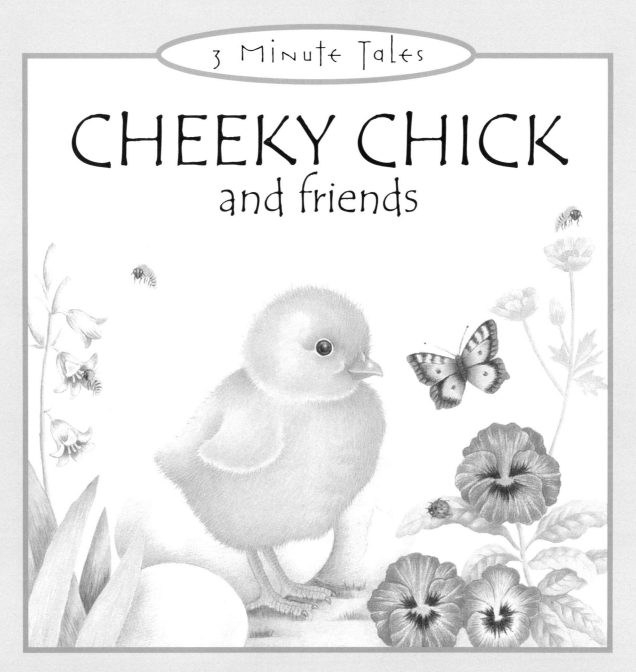

3 Minute Tales

CHEEKY CHICK
and friends

written by Caroline Repchuk   illustrated by Stephanie Boey

PIPPBROOK
BOOKS

Contents

Making a Splash!

Cheeky Chick

Little Chick Lost

"Stay close, Little Chick!" said Mummy
as they set out to visit Mrs Duck, who lived
on the pond. Little Chick tried to keep up
with Mummy, but there were so many
interesting things to look at that he soon
got lost in the long grass.

He was busy watching a shiny beetle climb a
blade of grass when a dark shadow fell over him.
Little Chick looked up to see a huge
dribbling mouth coming towards him!

It was a hungry fox! "Help!" he cried, looking around for somewhere to hide.

Just then, Spot the farm dog appeared and with
a great "WOOF!" he chased the fox away.
He was good at protecting the farm animals.
Mummy arrived flapping her wings.

"I told you to stay close," she said, tucking Little
Chick under her wing. And from then on, that
is just where Little Chick stayed!

THE DISAPPEARING EGGS

Mrs Hen had been sitting on her nest for
a long time, and she was tired and uncomfortable.
"I wish these eggs would hurry up and hatch!"
she said to herself crossly. But all she could
do was sit and wait, so she closed her eyes
and soon fell fast asleep.

She dreamed she was sitting on her nest when all of a sudden it started to wobble and shake. She was tipped this way and that, being poked and prodded as the eggs moved beneath her — someone was stealing her eggs! A deep voice was saying, "What lovely big ones!" It must be Mr Fox! She had to save her eggs!

Mrs Hen woke with a start, and looked
down at her nest in alarm. Sure enough,
her eggs had disappeared — but in their
place were six fluffy chicks, all prodding her
with their sharp little beaks.

"What lovely big ones!" said a deep voice nearby. It was Old Ned, the donkey. "Aren't they just!" said Mrs Hen with relief. "They were certainly worth the wait!"

Making a Splash!

One day, Mrs Hen and her chicks were
walking near the pond when Mrs Duck
swam by, followed by a line of ducklings.
The ducklings splashed around, ducking
and diving in the water. "Can we play in the
water too?" the chicks asked Mrs Hen.
"It looks like fun!"

"Oh no, dears," said Mrs Hen. "Chicks and water don't mix!" This made the chicks very miserable. "It's not fair!" they grumbled. "We wish we were ducklings!" On the way home, a big black cloud appeared and it started to rain. Soon the chicks' fluffy feathers were wet through.

They scurried back to the henhouse as fast as they could and arrived wet, cold and shivering. Soon they were snuggled in the cosy, warm straw, and their feathers were dry and fluffy again.

"Imagine being wet all the time!" said the chicks.
"Thank goodness we're not ducklings, after all!"

CHEEKY CHICK

Cheeky Chick was a playful little chick. He was always playing tricks on his brothers and sisters. He would hide in the long grass, then jump out at them in surprise, shouting "Boo!" One day they decided to get their own back. "Let's play hide and seek," they said.

They left Cheeky Chick to count to ten, while they all went to hide. Cheeky Chick hunted high and low for his brothers and sisters. He looked in all his favourite hiding places but they were nowhere to be found.

"Come out," he called. "I give up!"
But no one came.

So Cheeky Chick carried on looking.
He searched carefully all through the
farmyard, through the vegetable patch and
along the hedgerow at the edge of the
field. He even looked in the haystack,
which took a very long time, but there
was no sign of his brothers and sisters to
be found amongst the hay.

By now it was getting dark, and Cheeky
Chick was feeling scared and lonely.
"It's no use," he said to himself. "I'll have
to go home." He hurried to the henhouse
and opened the door. "Surprise!" came
a loud chorus. His brothers and sisters
had been hiding there all along! It was
a long time before Cheeky Chick played
tricks on them again.

The End